# DC SUPER FRIENDS™

# CRIME WAVE!

## BANTAM BOOKS

People are lining up
to see the world's
biggest pearl.

Aquaman cuts the ribbon
to open the show.
Superman, Batman
and all the people cheer!

Suddenly, water floods in.

The people leave.

The Super Friends

help the people.

Tentacles rise
out of the water!

It is a giant octopus!

Black Manta rides a
shark into the room.
Electric eels spark
around him.

Black Manta

picks up the pearl.

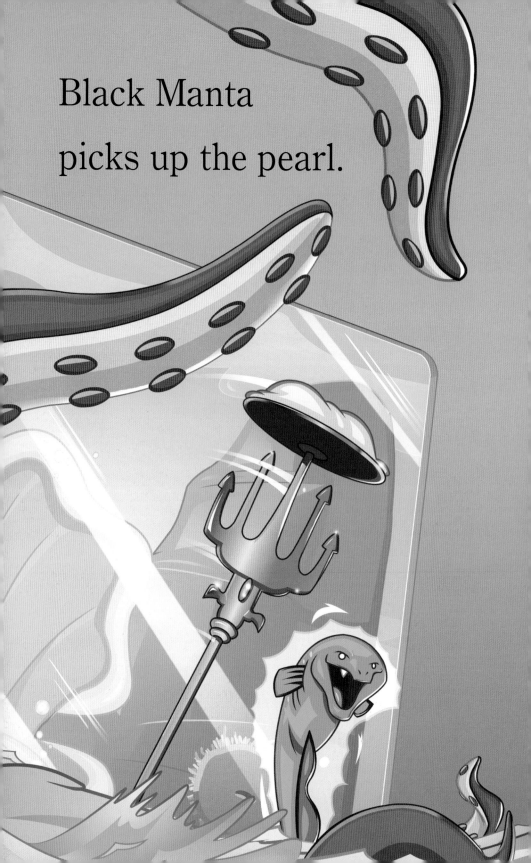

# He is stealing it!

The Super Friends stand
in Black Manta's way.

They will not let him
take the pearl.

Black Manta gives orders.
The shark, eels and
octopus attack
the Super Friends.

The electric eels
chase Batman.
He swings towards
the penguin pool.

The water is freezing.

The eels trap Batman!

# The shark snaps
# at Aquaman!

Black Manta clutches the pearl.

Superman fights
the octopus.

Black Manta

blasts Superman

with his lasers!

"I have won,"
Black Manta says.
"The pearl is mine!"

He forgets that Aquaman
can talk to sea creatures.

Aquaman tells the octopus that stealing is wrong.

The octopus sets

the Super Friends free.

Black Manta
falls backwards.
A giant oyster clamps
down on his foot.

Black Manta is trapped.

Batman gets the pearl.

The police take

Black Manta away.

Batman and Aquaman
put the pearl back.

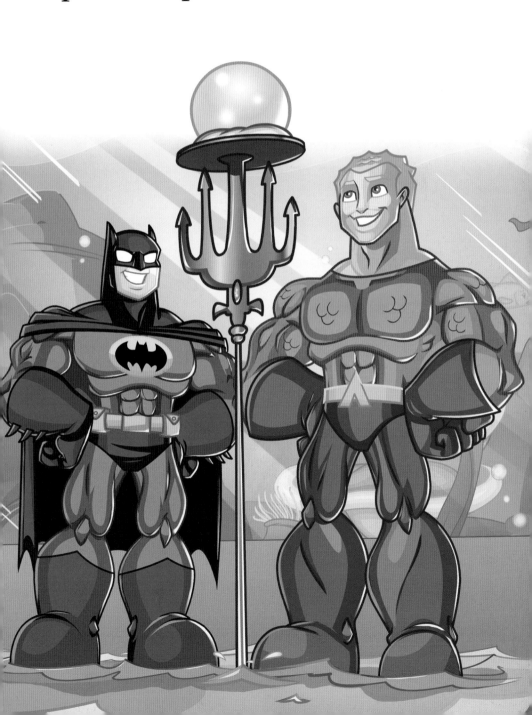

"I'm glad you are on
our side," Aquaman says.
"We don't have enough
Bat-Cuffs to arrest you!"